# SINCE THE FIRST DAY

## M. L. BUCHMAN

Buchman Bookworks

# SIGN UP FOR M. L. BUCHMAN'S NEWSLETTER TODAY

*and receive:*
*Release News*
*Free Short Stories*
*a Free Starter Library*

*Do it today. Do it now.*
*www.mlbuchman.com/newsletter*

# ALSO BY M. L. BUCHMAN

<u>THE NIGHT STALKERS</u>

MAIN FLIGHT

*The Night Is Mine*

*I Own the Dawn*

*Wait Until Dark*

*Take Over at Midnight*

*Light Up the Night*

*Bring On the Dusk*

*By Break of Day*

WHITE HOUSE HOLIDAY

*Daniel's Christmas*

*Frank's Independence Day*

*Peter's Christmas*

*Zachary's Christmas*

*Roy's Independence Day*

*Damien's Christmas*

AND THE NAVY

*Christmas at Steel Beach*

*Christmas at Peleliu Cove*

5E

*Target of the Heart*

*Target Lock on Love*

*Target of Mine*

<u>FIREHAWKS</u>
MAIN FLIGHT
*Pure Heat*
*Full Blaze*
*Hot Point*
*Flash of Fire*
*Wild Fire*
SMOKEJUMPERS
*Wildfire at Dawn*
*Wildfire at Larch Creek*
*Wildfire on the Skagit*

<u>DELTA FORCE</u>
MAIN FLIGHT
*Target Engaged*
*Heart Strike*
*Wild Justice*

<u>HENDERSON'S RANCH</u>
*Nathan's Big Sky*

<u>LOVE ABROAD B&B</u>
*Heart of the Cotswolds: England*

<u>WHERE DREAMS</u>
*Where Dreams are Born*
*Where Dreams Reside*
*Where Dreams Are of Christmas*
*Where Dreams Unfold*

*Where Dreams Are Written*

### E AGLE C OVE

*Return to Eagle Cove*

*Recipe for Eagle Cove*

*Longing for Eagle Cove*

*Keepsake for Eagle Cove*

### D EITIES A NONYMOUS

*Cookbook from Hell: Reheated*

*Saviors 101*

### D EAD C HEF

*Swap Out!*

*One Chef!*

*Two Chef!*

### SF/F T ITLES

*The Nara Reaction*

*Monk's Maze*

*The Me and Elsie Chronicles*

### S TRATEGIES FOR S UCCESS

*Managing Your Inner Artist / Writer*

*Don't miss a thing! Get a free starter library!*

*www.mlbuchman.com*

**1**

———

*Present Day, June 13, 2300 Hours (11 p.m. Panama Local Time)*

"It was a dark and stormy night!" Danny Corvo declared over the intercom as he fought the big helo's controls.

"Ho-ly crap!" Carmen's words were jarred out of her by the *Calamity Jane II* slamming into another squall line as if it was a solid wall. "Did Danny just make a jo-ke?"

He should have kept his mouth shut and just flown the damn helicopter.

The massive Chinook twin-rotor helicopter was getting battered by the tail end of a tropical storm they were using for cover on this training mission. The last thing to do under those conditions was to encourage Carmen.

"He did?" "What did I miss?" The other two gunners, probably woken up by Carmen's initial shout, chimed in like it was some special event they didn't want to miss. The Night Stalkers of the 160th Special Operations Aviation Regiment —SOAR—could sleep through almost anything. Except one of Carmen's cheery blasts.

"Do another one, Danny. Do another one," Carmen

pleaded like a toddler rather than being a definitely grown up, way hot redhead.

Captain Justin Roberts just grinned over at him from the pilot's seat. *You've stepped in it now,* written clear across what little Danny could see of his face. From the nose up, his features, like Danny's, were covered by his visor and helmet. It was an odd habit that made them turn to each other for a joke, but not during anything to do with flying. It wasn't as if they could see much. Most of his vision was blocked by the tactical view projected on the inside of his visor. The captain was a pale version of himself set beyond the display. He would have been invisible if they were over land, but at the moment they were beating ass toward an unsuspecting ship at sea with a team of Delta Force in the back. They had a Zodiac boat and were doing some exercise about taking down a cruise ship. Even storm-whipped, the sea didn't paint much on the tactical display.

Danny refocused on the inside of his visor. The weather was painted in large swaths of "don't go here" lying exactly in their path. Of course they'd just flown through a whole section just like it over the last half hour, so that didn't worry him. The horizon was a pale line across the center of his view with altitude, airspeed, and other critical readouts down the left. Dead ahead lay four symbols for ships: cargo and container carriers whose jobs were not being fun at the moment with the thirty-foot seas. And over the horizon, a small red rectangle pinpointing their target—a disabled luxury cruise liner, empty and under tow. Justin's wife Kara Moretti was back aboard the USS *Peleliu* and had the ship pinpointed for observation with her Gray Eagle drone quietly circling far above.

At least the Delta Force team was on their own circuit, so they'd still be able to sleep. It wasn't like Delta ever spoke to anyone else—ever—anyway. And not even to each other much that he'd seen.

"Please, please, please," Carmen wasn't going to let him go.

"Carmen. Begging. I like it," he took another run at being brave.

A fist thumped down on his shoulder which told him Carmen had shifted forward to the observer seat close behind the side-by-side pilots' seats. She was a very physical gal—which sent his thoughts in entirely the wrong direction. He supposed he was lucky, she'd probably have done it much harder if she'd known where his thoughts went so often.

"Picking on your pilot-in-command. Very dangerous, Carmen. *Picking* on the *PIC*," he emphasized the play on words, too late realizing that was probably too obvious.

"Why dangerous, Danny? It's just you."

"Maybe you're in the mood for a swim." Mission profile said stay low, the storm said stay high, he was a Night Stalker so he'd climbed a hundred feet above the waves, rather than the five thousand any rational Army pilot would have. The Night Stalkers flew at the edge of what he liked to call rational insanity. He'd become very comfortable with that over his five years with the 160th.

"Swim with the dashing Danny Corvo? Be sti-ill my heart." A microburst bounced them up fifty feet before he could compensate. Maybe staying a *little* farther from the waves would be a good idea. He took it as a sign from Mother Nature and stayed where she'd just bounced them to. They'd now be visible from farther away, not that radar would pick them out in this crap. The rain lashed so hard against the windshield and hull at their hundred-and-fifty-mile-an-hour speed, plus an obnoxious amount of wind velocity, that he could hear it despite his helmet. It was louder than the beastly big rotors of his Chinook.

"Swimming with you? That *totally* works for me."

A couple of the guys hooted encouragement. It was rare for anyone to banter with Carmen past the first round or two. Her wit was faster than an RPG and not much less dangerous.

He glanced at the engine readouts, even though that was Justin's job at the moment, with Carmen as a backup. The temperatures looked good, so the rain wasn't enough to drown the twin, five-thousand horsepower Lycoming engines. He turned his attention back to keeping them in the air.

And to picturing Carmen in a dark red bikini that matched her hair. Her fair skin and blue-green eyes the color of the tropical sea. Which at the moment was pitch black because it was almost midnight in a bitch of a storm a hundred-and-sixty miles off Panama. Almost midnight. It was hard to not smile even if it didn't really mean anything, except to him. He checked the dash clock, 2304 and counting.

"No, none of you mugs will *ever* see me in a bikini, so just stop thinking about that."

"Which plants the image firmly in my brain," Danny heaved on the thrust control along the left side of his seat to compensate for a sudden downdraft, but managed to stabilize at eighty feet above the waves before climbing back up.

"Ho-ly crap!" There was no air pocket to jar her words this time, so she did it herself. Damn but she was funny. "You guys heard that? You!" She poked him in the arm. "What did you do with our quiet and shy Danny Corvo?"

"I put him out to pasture where he belongs."

"Whoa!" "You were right, Carm." Vinnie and Raymond chimed in from the back.

"This *is* a passel of strange, ain't it," the captain agreed, his Texan accent far thicker than normal.

Danny liked flying with Justin Roberts. He was always cheery—even when everything was going to hell. Justin also gave him plenty of pilot-in-command time. He'd flown with a lot of commanders who just wanted you to sit your ass in the seat and leave them alone. However, egging Carmen on wasn't going to help anyth—

"Crazy weird," Carmen agreed. "It *sounds* like Danny. And I can see his cute little chin."

Just how every Army Special Operations guy wanted to be described by a hot soldier woman.

"*Where oh where has our Danny gone?*" The captain broke into song as he was apt to do at the drop of his cowboy hat.

Danny did his best to ignore it as they mangled the verse. At least until Carmen joined in with that sweet alto of hers for the refrain, "*Aliens done took him away.*"

Images of sticklike green men bearing rectal probes—and a particularly hard slam by the storm—definitely knocked the bikini-clad redhead out of his thoughts. Too bad. If his imagination was worth shit, she'd be damn cute in one.

## 2



*P*resent *Day, June 13, 2310 Hours (Panama Local Time)*

Danny had never joined in the singing aboard the *Calamity Jane II.* Carmen had teased him about that any number of times, to no avail. At least he'd stopped complaining about their choices of music, mostly.

He was such a quiet guy that he was hard to read. Even his laughs were quiet and his looks thoughtful. Though she could never tell quite what was going on behind those steady eyes.

"Why are you always such a serious guy?" The question was out before she could stop herself.

"Am I? I thought I was a happy-go-lucky leprechaun. Damn, and I was so close to finding me a pot of gold."

"Thought you said you were Portuguese." He looked it with those deep brown eyes, black hair, and sun-dark skin. He was also too handsome for words.

"That was the other Danny Corvo."

The others laughed, but Carmen was actually a little worried and found it hard to join in. This *wasn't* the Danny that she knew. He wasn't the kind of guy to crack under the stress of a flight no matter how horrid—to emphasize the point, her teeth clacked together sharply as the seat's shocks bottomed out hard in the next air pocket. But she couldn't imagine what was up with him.

She spent a few moments on the HUMS interface—as she'd been doing every five minutes or less of their ride through the storm. The helo's Health and Usage Monitoring Systems was reporting no problems, though she often *heard* problems before HUMS reported them. After nine years in Chinooks, the last two as a Night Stalker crew chief, the aircraft was in her blood. And no matter what the pilots thought, this was *her* bird. She was responsible for every nut, bolt, and signoff. The pilots just climbed aboard on occasion to do some flying.

She rested her hand against the inside of the hull and could feel it vibrating with the controlled violence of the twin Lycoming turbines spinning at fifteen thousand RPM and the uncontrolled violence of the storm. She could also feel every little shift in attitude and speed. It was unreal how fast Danny compensated for everything the storm could throw at him. Maybe he *was* some alternate version of himself.

For a while she simply rode along, enjoying the connection between them. The motion of the helo tied to the constant tiny corrections Danny made on the cyclic and thrust control. She couldn't see his feet on the rudder pedals in the dim light, but she could imagine the expert dance he used to keep fifteen tons of helicopter and crew headed toward their destination.

But she couldn't explain the sudden surfacing of a sense of humor. She liked knowing exactly what was going on with *all* of her equipment, and having a copilot suddenly develop a sense of humor was definitely throwing her.

Not that Danny was *hers*. He was actually the only one on the crew who hadn't at least made a pass at her. Of course Justin's had been after he was happily married to the lethal Kara Moretti, so it had been pure tease that she'd happily returned in kind.

But for her there'd always been something special about Danny.

She remembered her first day as a Night Stalker...which had been a night much like this one.

**3**

———

*Two Years Ago, June 14, 2320 Hours (Alabama Local Time)*
The downgraded hurricane had been beating the shit out of southern Alabama as a tropical storm when she'd gotten off the plane at Fort Rucker. It was a real "sicker" of a flight, everyone who wasn't a seasoned flier had been puking their guts out for the entire second half. Even some of the old hands lost it just from listening to all the others.

Carmen would admit that she'd regretted the gut bomb bacon-cheeseburger she'd had just before flight, but refused to be humiliated by seeing it again quite so soon.

She was a Night Stalker crew chief—at long last Fully Mission Qualified. And FMQ Night Stalkers didn't lose their shit because of a little lumpy air. Nonetheless glad to be on the ground, she shouldered her duffle, yanked on her helmet against the last of the six new inches of rain Alabama had gotten that day, and stepped off the flight squarely into a seriously handsome man's chest.

She flattened him right onto his ass.

"Boy, you sure are a pushover," she managed to keep her feet, barely. The rest of the flight began unloading to either side of them as the man she'd plowed into continued to lay in a puddle on the tarmac looking up at her. The storm cracked with lightning, revealing his bewildered expression, as fast-following thunder said the latest weather wasn't done with them yet.

"Sergeant Carmen Parker?"

She nodded and offered a hand, not that she was all that steady yet from the rough flight, but it seemed the least she could do.

He shook his head, either trying to clear it or to say no.

But before she could withdraw her hand, he'd taken it and let her help him to his feet.

"Thanks."

"This is your definition of personal space?" The man stood just inches away, their clasped hands the only thing keeping them apart. So close that it was hard to tell, even in the light spilling out of a nearby hangar, if he was really as handsome as her first impression.

"Not really," he took a step back, then another. He was mighty slow about letting go of her hand though, which was kind of sweet. No complaints from her: muscled, Latino, five-ten to her five-six, and one of those guys who was surprisingly handsome but probably didn't realize it. His easy smile lit his face without doing anything more than saying, "Hi!" No "Hey, baby!" or "Nice to meet you, hot stuff!"

She'd never minded guys flirting with her—especially because she could kick the ass of anyone who overstepped the bounds. But Danny was like the perfect straight man for her teasing. Maybe even too straight because it didn't seem to phase him in the slightest.

"I'm Danny Corvo, the copilot on your new assignment." Then he shook the hand he'd still been holding and let go.

One more step back and "proper personal space" was reestablished.

"Lead on and I will follow," she put a lot of sass into it just to test him.

"This way," he waved toward an electric golf cart of all things. Truly a straight man, unless he was gay. No, she'd seen where his eyes had traveled, however briefly. Then he turned and she saw that he was soaked from butt to brain because of his dunk in the puddle. Yet he made no complaints, no tease. Not even a decent grumble. Weird.

4



*Present Day, June 13, 2330 Hours (Panama Local Time)*

Even after two years, Danny never quite understood what had hit him that day. The shock of Carmen striding down the flight's ramp like she owned Fort Rucker had been visceral. When she'd slammed into him it had become physical as well. He'd had no extra attention span to even try to recover—he'd simply toppled over.

He'd looked up at the vision of Woman standing over him. Serious curves under a black t-shirt and camo pants. The finer qualities of her figure only emphasized by the heavy duffle she wore backpack-style, pulling her shoulders back. Topped off by a Night Stalkers helmet painted with a flamenco dancer in a flirty red skirt on the side.

Carmen from the opera by Bizet.

It had unquestionably been the new crew member he'd come to fetch from the transport flight, but all he'd been able to do was lie in the puddle and stare as she sassed him.

*Real smooth.*

In two years, he also hadn't figured out what he should have done differently. You didn't just grab a woman like

Carmen Parker, her inner strength showed as clearly as her figure from the first moment. In the way she walked, in the way she carried herself, in the way she held focus on what mattered to the exclusion of all else. If she had to walk out into a hail of gunfire to help an injured aboard, she did it without a cringe. If some meathead tried to grab her, she laid him out flat, then dusted her hands of him and went back to whatever she'd been doing. Nothing touched her when turned on that laser focus—which was pretty much all the time.

A particularly heavy squall line in the storm had him climbing up to five hundred feet before they hit it. Sure enough, the solid wall of water that this tropical storm called "rain" took ten percent out of his engines—water just didn't burn very well no matter how much Jet-A fuel you let loose with the throttle.

He kept an eye on the engines as he came out the other side. The Lycomings only took a few seconds to clear their throats and climb back to full power. Damn but he loved this bird. Almost as much as he loved—

Useless thought. Carmen Parker wasn't for the likes of him.

But he couldn't think of anything other than her strength. And her boundless joy and humor—she was funny enough for any five other people combined. That was one of the main reasons he kept his mouth shut. Anything he came up with was going to sound lame next to the cool shit Carmen could deliver on no notice.

Once the engine temperatures had restabilized at fifteen-hundred degrees, he descended back onto profile. Their target ship was well out of the storm now, shifting into the calmer waters close under Panama's mountainous coastline, but he angled in a little deeper into the storm to get them as close as possible while under its cover. Night Stalkers method: push every training opportunity to the limit and maybe, just maybe, you'll have the chance to survive the real thing.

Danny remembered the day things had changed between them. It had nothing to do with mud puddles that had almost earned him a "Danny the Duck" nickname or his soaking flightsuit.

At least not one soaked with water.

5

___

*One year ago, June 13, 2340 Hours (Yemen Local Time)*

Justin was flying right-seat as usual. But a new copilot flew in Danny's seat—out for an indoctrination run. He was FMQ in the tiny MH-6M Little Bird helicopters. A Little Bird had four seats, but you didn't want to be one of the folks in the back seat, compared to the fifty-plus troops that his Chinook could carry in addition to her five crew. Weighing in at less than a ton apiece, a Chinook could lift fifteen Little Birds without breaking a sweat. But the company commander wanted every one of their pilots to at least have a feel for the capabilities of each airframe type that SOAR flew. And what Pete Napier ordered, nobody messed with.

So, while the copilot had stretched his flight legs over the nighttime Gulf of Aden, Danny had been relegated to the back to see what the crew chiefs did for a living.

"We do all kinds of cool shit back here," Carmen had set them to Intercom Channel 4 so that they wouldn't bother anyone else as she gave him the tour.

"Such as?"

She pointed to Vinnie and Raymond sacked out on the hard steel deck.

"You sleep?"

"You guys up there are just giving us a rocking cradle ride—"

The trainee was slamming the Chinook through a turn worthy of an F-35 Lightning II fighter jet, forcing both of them to hang on so that they didn't tumble about the cargo bay like pinballs.

"No hostiles around," Carmen didn't even break her speech as the helo slid to a halt in mid-air and did a full spin —not an easy trick in a Chinook, which he flubbed the first couple times. "No gunnery practice to do. We might as well grab some shuteye back here. I can run this whole sweet bird by myself."

"Except for flying it," Danny tried to carve out some territory for his role.

"Pilots! Feh!" Carmen wiggled her fingers at him. Then she started guiding him through an in-flight systems check. Every five minutes this, every ten that, and a full tour of the bird's interior along with a dozen systems checks every half hour. She waved the checklists at him, though it was clear she didn't need them. They were at least as long as the pilot's set. "Then when we're on the ground..." she'd pulled out an even bigger set of checklists.

Carmen had always humbled him. Now he was discovering that she was more daunting than he'd thought. If he could just somehow—

"Alert Status One! Alert Status One!" slammed in over the primary intercom channel. Vinnie and Raymond bolted to their feet as if electroshocked.

"You!" Carmen had jabbed a finger against his arm. "You stay attached to my hip or you'll get run over."

"I should—" he pointed forward, but knew he wasn't needed. All through Carmen's tour he'd been aware of the rapidly growing competence of the new pilot as Justin ran him through the paces. A Chinook was no Black Hawk and trading positions in mid-flight was actually possible. But Justin didn't call him forward and he supposed he agreed. Nothing like being at the helm during action to really learn what it took. And Justin Roberts could handle almost anything solo if he had to.

Their little training sortie became a crash-priority evac for a mixed team of the 75th Rangers and Delta. By the time they hit the Yemeni shoreline, a heavily-armed DAP Black Hawk and a Combat Search and Rescue Hawk had joined them as well.

Carmen and Vinnie each shot a few test rounds out of their side-facing miniguns then began checking their personal weapons. He did the same. Raymond went to the rear of the cargo bay and began rigging his ramp gun, even though the ramp was still closed tightly, shutting out the night.

They came in on the terrorist camp low and fast.

Danny presently had the crews' tactical feed on his visor rather than his normal pilot's version. Far more information about the engines and systems performance—next to nothing about the terrain except in the broadest strokes. The threat monitors were soon piecing together the situation. Small arms fire raking along the ground in a vast, back-and-forth interplay of flying death.

The DAP Hawk climbed above the camp and answered back hard.

It was so disorienting when their missile slammed down on one of the compounds—he hadn't known it was coming like he normally would have.

The DAP Hawk gun platform was raining down hell. The CSAR bird was hanging back in case it was needed, and their Chinook was head-on into the fray. On the ground, one Black Hawk was burning fiercely and another was being protected by more soldiers than the one bird could carry out. No...soldiers and several rescued hostages.

Justin—Danny could feel the familiar flight control of the captain taking control—eased the *Calamity Jane II* toward the men on the ground surrounding the beleaguered Black Hawk.

More and more of the fire was directed upward at the DAP Hawk dancing and spinning overhead, which eased the burden here on the ground. Justin got them landed close beside the waiting troops.

The instant the ramp was down, troops stormed aboard. Not all of them were soldiers. Three hostages, two clearly American and the third sounding Japanese, looked battered, confused, and disbelieving at their sudden rescue. There were no hostiles as prisoners. Some operations just didn't call for that.

Several soldiers came aboard with a rifle in one hand and an arm over a buddy's shoulders. Most of those hit the relative safety of the cargo bay and collapsed.

Carmen's station was on the side away from the action—whereas Vinnie's side gun was unleashing a near constant roar of four thousand rounds a minute—so the two of them grabbed med kits and began helping the worst of the wounded.

The hull rattled with small arms fire. Sometimes a double-smack as a bullet penetrated one side and splatted against the other. Soldiers were hitting the deck as the windows were shot out.

He'd strapped off two legs with tight bandages and was

pressing down on a shoulder wound as they lifted. Less than twenty feet in the air, the helo...flinched. Forty thousand pounds of helo wasn't supposed to flinch.

Critical system failure or—

"Corvo!" Justin's voice called him forward. But if he let go on this guy's wound, he'd bleed out before anyone else could get to him.

"You!" Danny shouted a nearby soldier. "Pressure! Here!"

The man was injured himself. "Can't you get the medic?"

Danny tapped the downed man's armband—a red cross bathed in blood. "He *is* your medic."

The guy looked positively green, but placed his hands onto the wounded medic's shoulder.

"If you're gonna be sick, turn to the side so that you aren't sick on him." Then Danny scrambled forward over the bodies of both the wounded and exhausted. The helo was wavering, making him stagger like a drunk on his way forward.

There was no question about what the problem was when he got to the front. The forward windscreen was shattered and the trainee copilot hung limply in his harness.

"Carmen!" Danny shouted out and hoped they still had their private intercom set up.

"Can't see shit!" Justin complained.

Danny saw why. There was blood trickling down his face and it had covered both his eyes. It wasn't gushing, but it wasn't good. The captain couldn't wipe it away because he needed both hands on the controls.

In moments Carmen was at his shoulder.

He gave the blinded Justin moment-by-moment directions on the flight controls while Carmen helped him lever the trainee out of the copilot's seat. He tried not to be too squeamish as he slid in to sit in another man's blood.

Finally buckled into the seat's harness, he shouted out, "I have control."

Justin slumped down—having kept them aloft and steady on sheer nerve—and cursed. "Hell of a way to run a rodeo."

Danny flipped to the pilot's view and the full tactical hell of the situation slammed in. Much of the camp was burning. Men were down everywhere, though he didn't see any American bodies—no telltale infrared tabs that would have glowed like searchlights in his night-vision display.

Three soldiers ran from the second Black Hawk—now also burning brightly—toward the back of the Chinook. Danny eased the tail back down. One stumbled and fell—and didn't get up.

From the copilot's raised seat, he spotted the problem. Someone had picked up an AK-47 from a fallen Yemeni and shot the Delta Force operator at least a dozen times from behind, mostly in the leg.

Danny snapped the position lock on the thrust control to free up his left hand. Yanking out his Glock sidearm, he shot twice. Once to blow out his side window, and once to shoot the Yemeni with the AK-47 in the heart.

The shooter collapsed.

Danny slapped the sidearm back in his holster and began easing back down for the wounded Delta.

"CSAR 1. We've got him," a woman's voice. Someone jumped out of the medevac bird and rushed over to the fallen soldier crawling along and dragging one leg.

"Roger. *Calamity Jane II* aloft."

He pulled up and back to clear the CSAR bird and the two grounded and burning Black Hawks. Then got them the hell out of Dodge as soon as the CSAR bird was aloft.

As he was pulling away, he finally got perspective on the

shooter he'd just downed and the man he'd taken the AK-47 from in the first place. The shooter was half the size of the dead man.

"I just shot a kid." Probably dropped him on his dad's body.

Carmen, who'd been treating Justin now collapsed in his seat, spun to face him.

He remembered the feel of her comforting hand on his shoulder for a long time after she'd turned back to bandaging the captain.

No one else had heard. He also left that part out of the after-action debriefing.

## 6

---

*Present Day, June 13, 2350 Hours (Panama Local Time)*

Carmen did a full inspection and systems check as Danny continued to fight them through the storm. A couple of the Deltas were awake. It was a strange team. Three women, four men. She'd never seen a female Delta before and here was a whole clump of them. A gaggle of geese. A flock of ewes. An incoming disaster of Deltas? What would it be like to be a woman who kicked butt at a Delta level? She'd miss her Chinook too much, but the three women looked beyond cool.

One of the guy Deltas called her over.

"Oh. My. God!" Carmen slapped a hand to her chest and put her wrist to her forehead. "I'm gonna faint. It only took four hours for one of the silent warriors to acknowledge that they weren't the only people on this flight." Then she collapsed onto one of the Zodiac's pontoons and fell upside down into the bottom of the boat to sprawl at his feet.

Several of the Deltas startled awake, inspected her strangely for a moment, then went back to sleep.

"Got a question for you, once you're done playing the lead role from a Bizet opera."

"What are you talking about?" She continued laying upside down, but raised her head to inspect him. He was handsome, but she was feeling oddly self-conscious about teasing him, which wasn't like her. She teased everybody—except Danny since that night he'd shot the kid.

"The opera *Carmen*. The dazzling man killer."

"There's an opera named after me?" As if she didn't have Carmen the gypsy dancer emblazoned on the side of her helmet. "How cool is that? Dazzling man killer—perfect fit. Are you my next victim? This should be fun."

The guy looked at his watch, typical Delta.

She flipped around until she was upright once again.

"How would you take down a cruise ship?"

Delta operators had no sense of humor.

"Couple-a Hellfire missiles at the waterline?"

The discussion went on for a few minutes, but her thoughts were on why Danny was acting so strangely. She left the Deltas sitting in their rubber boat in the cargo bay talking about it and drifted back forward.

She ended up close behind the two pilots' seats. She didn't usually ride in the observer's chair, but the memory of the two storms—the present one and the one in which she'd met Danny—had drawn her back to the front.

Her last two years aboard the *Calamity Jane II* stood out so much more clearly than the five prior years in the regular Army or the two years of additional training to become a Night Stalker.

No, that wasn't all of it. Each moment *with Danny* stood out. The good and the bad. The smooth perfection of how he'd flown them out of that battle, despite a windshield so star-cracked that he could only fly by peaking out of the bullet holes marking where unfriendly fire had wounded the captain and killed the last person in that seat, despite the shot-up hydraulics that had forced him to wrestle the massive helo by brute force, all while having just shot a kid. The quiet ease with which he sat back at a hangar barbeque: beer in his hand, smile on his face, just watching the goings on, watching her...

Watching *her.*

With the same look as the moment she'd plowed him ass over teakettle into a mud puddle. A look she'd never forgotten, but couldn't understand. Unless...

Her throat was suddenly dry.

She leaned forward and rested a hand on his shoulder.

He flipped to Intercom Channel 4. One, she finally realized, that they'd shared often for privacy. Privacy? They were just on the same crew together, why did they need a private channel? Yet they had one. Sometimes back-enders (her and the other two crew chiefs) shared Channel 2 so as not to disturb the pilots, but usually the whole team stayed on Channel 1. Danny was the only one she had a "private" channel with.

He waited for her in silence as he held tight control of the bucking bronc that was the Chinook in the storm.

"Danny?"

"Carmen," his voice was "normal" Danny. Not substitute Danny Corvo. No joke or humor. Once again her straight man was there.

"Why..." she couldn't quite bring herself to confront her question directly. "...why don't you ever sing?"

He chuckled with the warmth of a caress, accepting the evasion. "Tone deaf. I've been told that I sing like a choking hyena."

"You can't be that bad."

"Sadly, sometime when we're alone, I can prove it. Besides, if I don't sing it lets me hear you better."

And now they were back to the inexplicable attack of nerves she was having. She checked the HUMS again, but the helo's health was just fine despite the thrashing of the wind and rain. It was hers that was in doubt.

"You're still wondering what I did with the real Danny Corvo?"

"Well…" Carmen took a deep breath and plunged in. "You've always been the straight man. Mr. AJ Squared Away."

"That's sailor talk. What would that be in Army-speak? Mr. Shiny Shithook pilot?" A shithook was slang for an Army Chinook helicopter.

"See! That! That isn't the Danny I know."

"But it is," he whispered as she watched him slew their Chinook around a particularly dense cloud that blanketed a whole section of the radar screen. It was so strange to be having this conversation while he was busy and Captain Roberts was sitting about a foot away, oblivious to everything.

"How? The Danny Corvo I know doesn't joke or tease or—"

"Okay. No tease. There's this beach I know, just down from my grandfather's house, called Praia da Marinha, in southern Portugal on the Atlantic. Just a few hundred kilometers from where the opera about you is set. Warm. Soft sand with tall cliffs, sea arches, caves. It is one of the most beautiful places I've ever been. I would take you there. Maybe you'd wear a red bikini. Same color as your beautiful hair."

"Already said, no bikini." It was lame, but it was the best defense she had against such a beautiful vision.

"How about a flamenco dancer's dress?"

She sat back and glared at the side of his helmet. That didn't sound like Danny either—no matter how much she liked the sound of it. Her and Danny off somewhere sunny. They'd—

*Her and Danny?*

Her personal HUMS system should be flashing red lights and alert sirens.

"Why didn't you ever say any of this before?" She wanted to grab and shake him. Would have if he wasn't flying.

"Tired of waiting."

"For me?"

"No, me. To be brave."

She wasn't sure if she'd ever met a braver man. Heavy gunfire, his captain wounded, rattled because he'd shot an underage terrorist, and *then* started to re-land his helo to retrieve the wounded Delta. "What in the world do you have trouble being brave about?"

"Not yet."

"What do you mean, not yet?"

"Two more minutes."

She glanced at the mission clock on the helo's main console.

2358.

Too stubborn and maybe too unnerved to ask why, she folded her arms and waited in silence.

She could feel Danny smiling as he flew. They reached the edge of the storm closest to the cruise ship where the Delta operators would soon be simulating an attack. He banked hard, out of the interminable pounding of the storm and into clear air. The wind calmed and even the sky above began clearing as they raced away from the storm. He slid back down toward the sea.

They were the two longest minutes of her life.

It finally flipped to four zeros.

"A new day. Now give."

"Not just any day."

"Danny..." she knew she was grinding her teeth.

"June Fourteenth." He waited.

She didn't get it.

"Two years ago today..."

The date was ringing a bell. It was...the day she'd joined the crew of *Calamity Jane II*. It was the second anniversary of... "Oh shit!"

"Yep! Two years ago you bowled me over and I've never recovered."

"Two years," she could barely breathe.

"It's our second collision-anniversary."

"What was the first?" And then she knew and was sorry she'd asked.

"The kid."

She'd made a point of tracking Danny down afterward at the carrier. He'd been sitting on an old tire in a back corner of the hangar deck, just staring out at the dark sea. She didn't remember what they'd talked about, not much of anything. But they'd sat for hours and she remembered his brief hug and his whispered "Thanks" when the sun rose over the Gulf of Aden.

Again his silent patience while she processed things. He understood her. Everyone else she'd been able to brush off with a joke or a flirt.

Not Danny.

He'd stuck by her. Encouraged her. Made sure she knew she was welcome from that first day. In the Night Stalkers you didn't need someone to push you to excel, everyone did that. Everyone set their standards so high that you just wanted to strive to keep up with them. She was no different. Nor was Danny.

One of the Delta couples came up with a change in the deployment for the exercise. They ran it by her and the two pilots. They'd decided to add a maneuver to the simulated attack.

After she told them it was technically possible—though she kept to herself that it was bat-shit crazy, making it perfect for Delta—they cleared the last of the details with Danny before returning to the cargo bay.

Danny had been her quiet place. Somehow he let her know that she was okay even when she was too tired to speak or too sick of the unending supply of terrorist nut jobs.

He was...the man she didn't know how to live without. When she'd hauled the trainee pilot's body out of the copilot seat, she'd only been able to be thankful that he'd been sitting there rather than Danny. It was a guilty thought, but it ran deep. She would step in front of the bullet herself if it made sure he was still in the world afterward.

"Fifteen minutes to target," Danny announced on the PA.

No response. She turned, and could see that the Delta operators were completing their final prep. Silent warriors indeed.

Danny had stayed silent about his attraction to her. So carefully silent that she'd assumed he wasn't attracted at all, making her keep her own mouth shut about how much she'd been attracted to him. Shut enough that she'd almost buried the feeling. Just kept on being Carmen—wild, funny, in your face.

But now she knew, now she understood that smile on Danny's face. He always laughed with her jokes, but he also saw the quiet person inside her too. It wasn't Carmen the flashy gypsy dancer he was attracted to. It was Carmen Parker, lead crew chief of the Night Stalkers' Chinook *Calamity Jane II.*

"Danny?"

"Carmen," he said it exactly the way he had before.

"You really feel that way?" Was if even possible she could be so lucky?

He twisted all the way around to look at her for just a brief moment. "Really."

She wished she could see his eyes behind the visor, but she could see his smile, and that was enough. With Danny Corvo that was everything and it always would be.

He turned back to flying and she hustled back to make sure the Delta team was ready for the drop. She lowered the rear ramp and peeked out into the night.

The sea was calm, twenty minutes and sixty miles from the storm's closest approach.

The sky was clear.

All the flying ahead wouldn't be smooth. There'd be more gut wrenchers, but she knew, she just *knew* that they'd get through it all together.

Justin started humming a song over the intercom. Vinnie picked it up with his low baritone and she found herself joining in on the melody before she caught herself.

"What the hell?"

"Y'all amaze me," Justin Roberts spoke over the intercom, his Texas cranked up to full mud-thick. "Like y'all think that simply going up to little old Intercom 4 makes you private somehow. Rest of us tumbled to that trick about six months back. Let me just say, 'bout time, you two." And then he swung back into the music.

"Does this mean I'm going to have to buy a goddamn bikini?"

There was a mass chorus of, "Yes!" without breaking the rhythm.

"Then all you boys are buying goddamn thongs. Beach wedding."

There were laughs over the channel.

"Love you, gypsy dancer. Since the first day," Danny slipped in quietly between the words.

And he was right. "Since the first day," she echoed back.

Then, as she helped the Delta operators launch their boat out into the night, she joined in the chorus.

*The hills (skies, Danny stuck in) are alive, with the sound of music.*

"They were right you know," she whispered between the words. "You do sing like a choking hyena."

He only sang louder.

It took an entire chorus before she could stop laughing with joy and join back in.

# WILD JUSTICE (COMING FALL 2017)

DELTA FORCE ROMANCE NOVEL #3

"Who the hell are you, sister? And how did you get here?"

"Holy crap!"

What kind of woman said *crap* when unexpectedly facing a sniper rifle at point blank range?

"And not your sister," she gained points for a quick recovery. "Now get that rifle out of my face, Jarhead."

*Ouch!* That was low. Duane Jenkins wasn't some damned Marine. Not even ex-Marine. He was ex-75th Rangers of the US Army, now two years in Delta Force. And as an operator for The Unit, that put him way above any other soldier no matter what the dudes in SEAL Team 6 thought about it. That also didn't explain who he'd just found here in *the* perfect sniper position overlooking General Raul Estevan Aguado's encampment.

The low hill, shadowed by banana and mango trees in the twilight of the late afternoon sun above the Venezuelan jungle, overlooked the heavily guarded camp a half-mile away. It had taken him over fifteen hours to scout out this one perfect gap between the too-damn-tall trees that made up this sweaty place and, with just twenty meters to go, he'd spotted her heavily camouflaged form lying among the leaves. It had taken him another half hour to cover that distance without drawing her attention.

This place was worse than Atlanta in the summer. The red earth had been driven so deep into his pores from crawling over the ground that he wondered if his skin color was permanently changed to rust red.

Why the hell did evil bastards like Aguado have to come from such places?

*More immediate problem, dude. Stay focused.*

The woman's accent was American with a thin overlay that matched her Spanish features—full-lipped with dark eyebrows and darker eyes, which was about all he could tell through her camo paint—and she wasn't supposed to be here. No one was.

"Keeping you in my sights until I get some answers," Duane kept his H&K MSG90 A2 rifle aimed right at the bridge of her nose—a straight-through spine cutter if he had to take her down. It would be serious overkill, as the weapon was rated to lethal past eight hundred meters and they were whispering at each other from less than two meters apart. With the silencer, his weapon would be even quieter than their whispers, but he hadn't spent the last sixteen hours crawling into position to have her death cry give him away. If she so much as squawked as she went down, every goddamn bird in the jungle would light off, giving away his presence.

She sighed and nodded toward her own rifle that rested on the ground in front of her.

He shifted his focus—though not his aim—then let out a very low whistle of appreciation. A G28. Even his team hadn't gotten their hands on the latest entry into the US

Army's sniper arsenal yet. Not quite the same accuracy as his own weapon but six inches shorter, several pounds lighter, and far more flexible to configure. A whole generational leap forward. Richie, his team's tech, would be geeking out right about now. The fact that he wasn't here to see it almost made Duane smile.

"A Heckler & Koch G28. What's your point, sister?" He drawled it out for Richie's sake, who'd be listening in on Duane's radio. Then the implications sunk in. If his Delta Force team couldn't get these yet, then who could? Whatever else this sniper was, she would be tied to one of the three US Special Mission Units: Delta, SEAL Team 6, or the combat controllers of the Air Force's 24th STS.

Or The Activity.

That fit.

The Intelligence Support Activity served the other three Special Mission Units. If she was with the Activity…that was seriously hot. It meant she was both one of the top intel specialists anywhere and a lethal fighter. And that meant that *she'd* been the one to put out the call that had sent him here. That at least answered why she was in his spot. It also said a lot that she hadn't taken any of several easier to reach locations that were almost as good.

"About time you caught a clue. Welcome to the game." She picked up her rifle as if his wasn't still aimed at her. Very chill. "A little slow there."

"Hey, they don't call me 'The Rock' for nothing," Duane lowered his barrel until it was pointed into the dirt. "They actually call me that becau—"

The moment his weapon was down, he suddenly was staring down the dark hole of the G28's silencer.

"Uh…"

"The Rock certainly isn't because you are a towering

black movie star. It must be for your thick head."

Duane swallowed carefully, unable to shift his focus from into the barrel of her weapon to see if the safety was on or not.

"He spells his name differently. He's Dwayne 'The Rock' with a w and a y. I'm more normal, D-u-a-n-e T-h-e R-o-c-k."

"M-o-u-s-e," she finished for him. Because of course they'd both been kids when the *The All-New Mickey Mouse Club* had been airing.

He couldn't help laughing, quietly, despite their positions—him still staring down the barrel of her weapon.

"Normal is not what I need here," the woman sighed and there was the distinct click of her reengaging the safety on her rifle.

"Only thing normal about me is my name."

"Prove it," she turned her weapon once more toward the camp half a kilometer away through the trees.

Duane breathed out slowly and spent the next minute easing the last two meters toward her. Having the camp in view meant that one of their spotters could see them as well, if the bad guys were damned lucky. He and the woman both wore ghillie suits—that's why he'd gotten so close before he spotted her. The suits were made of open-weave cloth liberally decorated with leaves and twigs so that the two of them looked like little more than the jungle floor. He'd dragged his on backcountry jungle roads for twenty miles to make sure he smelled like the jungle as well. Having a jaguar notice his ass wouldn't exactly brighten up his day.

Even their rifles were well camouflaged except for either end of the spotting scopes and the very tips of the barrels. If he hadn't recently been lusting over the new specs, he wouldn't have recognized her Heckler & Koch G28 at all in its disguise.

Getting into position as a sniper took a patience that only the most highly trained could achieve. A female sniper? That was a rare find indeed. The two women on his Delta team were damned fine shooters, but he and Chad were the snipers of the crew. A female sniper from The Activity? This just kept getting better and better. He'd pay a fair wage to know what she really looked like beneath the ghillie and all the face paint.

At long last he lay beside her, close enough that he would have felt her body heat if not for the smothering sauna of his ghillie suit.

"Let's see what y'all are up to down there."

The general's camp was a simple affair in several ways. The enclosure was a few hundred meters across. An old-school fence of wooden stakes driven into the ground, each a small tree trunk three meters high with sharpened points upward. Not that the points mattered because of the razor wire looped along the top. Guard shacks every hundred meters—four total. The towers straddled the fence. Not a good idea. The structure should have been entirely behind the wall to protect it from attack. Unless...

"You got a name, darling?" Lying beside her, Duane could tell that they were of similar height. Her hands were fine, though her body was hidden by the ghillie.

"Yes."

"That's nice. Always good to have a name," Duane could play that game just as well as the next person. He turned to his attention to the camp. "Our friendly general isn't worried about attack from the outside or he'd have built his towers differently. He's worried about keeping people inside."

*Available for pre-order July 2017*

# ABOUT THE AUTHOR

M.L. Buchman started the first of, what is now over 50 novels and as many short stories, while flying from South Korea to ride his bicycle across the Australian Outback. Part of a solo around the world trip that ultimately launched his writing career.

All three of his military romantic suspense series—The Night Stalkers, Firehawks, and Delta Force—have had a title named "Top 10 Romance of the Year" by the American Library Association's *Booklist*. NPR and Barnes & Noble have named other titles "Top 5 Romance of the Year." In 2016 he was a finalist for Romance Writers of America prestigious RITA award. He also writes: contemporary romance, thrillers, and fantasy.

Past lives include: years as a project manager, rebuilding and single-handing a fifty-foot sailboat, both flying and jumping out of airplanes, and he has designed and built two houses. He is now making his living as a full-time writer on the Oregon Coast with his beloved wife and is constantly amazed at what you can do with a degree in Geophysics. You may keep up with his writing and receive a free starter e-library by subscribing to his newsletter at: www.mlbuchman.com

# ALSO BY M. L. BUCHMAN

<u>THE NIGHT STALKERS</u>

MAIN FLIGHT

*The Night Is Mine*

*I Own the Dawn*

*Wait Until Dark*

*Take Over at Midnight*

*Light Up the Night*

*Bring On the Dusk*

*By Break of Day*

WHITE HOUSE HOLIDAY

*Daniel's Christmas*

*Frank's Independence Day*

*Peter's Christmas*

*Zachary's Christmas*

*Roy's Independence Day*

*Damien's Christmas*

AND THE NAVY

*Christmas at Steel Beach*

*Christmas at Peleliu Cove*

5E

*Target of the Heart*

*Target Lock on Love*

*Target of Mine*

**FIREHAWKS**

MAIN FLIGHT

*Pure Heat*

*Full Blaze*

*Hot Point*

*Flash of Fire*

*Wild Fire*

SMOKEJUMPERS

*Wildfire at Dawn*

*Wildfire at Larch Creek*

*Wildfire on the Skagit*


**DELTA FORCE**

MAIN FLIGHT

*Target Engaged*

*Heart Strike*

*Wild Justice*


**HENDERSON'S RANCH**

*Nathan's Big Sky*


**LOVE ABROAD B&B**

*Heart of the Cotswolds: England*


**WHERE DREAMS**

*Where Dreams are Born*

*Where Dreams Reside*

*Where Dreams Are of Christmas*

*Where Dreams Unfold*

*Where Dreams Are Written*

### EAGLE COVE

*Return to Eagle Cove*

*Recipe for Eagle Cove*

*Longing for Eagle Cove*

*Keepsake for Eagle Cove*

### DEITIES ANONYMOUS

*Cookbook from Hell: Reheated*

*Saviors 101*

### DEAD CHEF

*Swap Out!*

*One Chef!*

*Two Chef!*

### SF/F TITLES

*The Nara Reaction*

*Monk's Maze*

*The Me and Elsie Chronicles*

### STRATEGIES FOR SUCCESS

*Managing Your Inner Artist / Writer*

*Don't miss a thing! Get a free starter library!*

*www.mlbuchman.com*

## SIGN UP FOR M. L. BUCHMAN'S NEWSLETTER TODAY

*and receive:*
*Release News*
*Free Short Stories*
*a Free Starter Library*

*Do it today. Do it now.*
*www.mlbuchman.com/newsletter*

www.ingramcontent.com/pod-product-compliance
Lightning Source LLC
Chambersburg PA
CBHW030026200726
48283CB00012B/1342